Sid Did It!

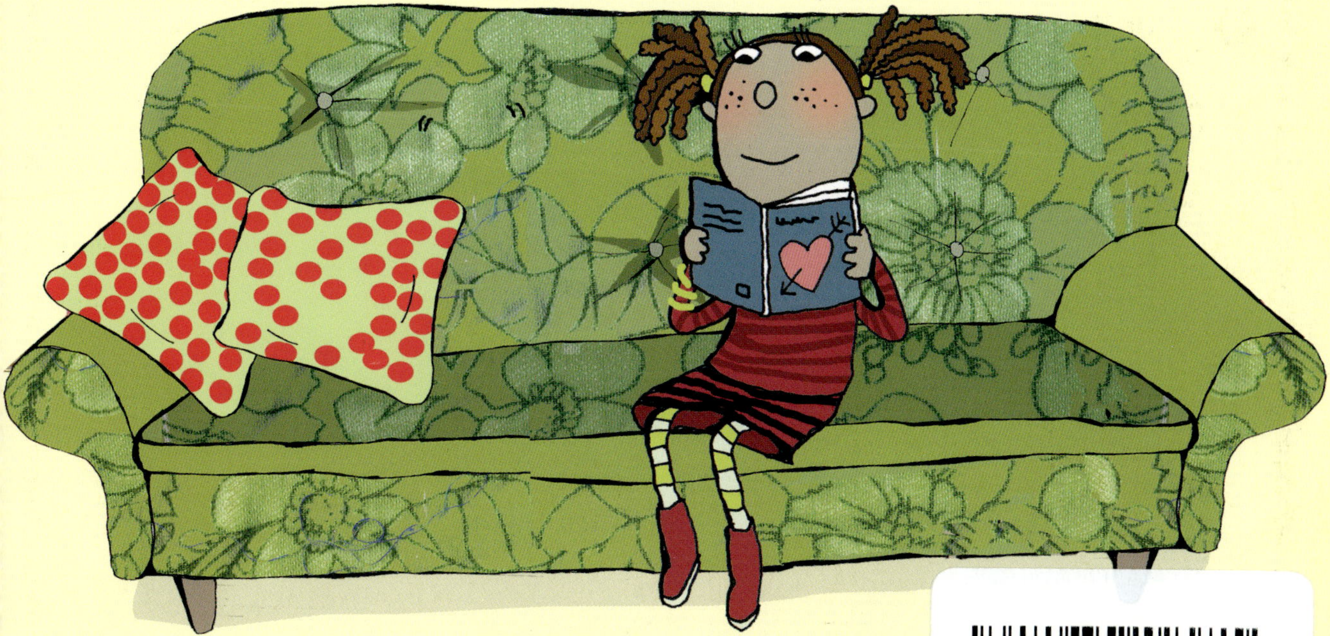

Written by Jeanne Willis

Illustrated by Jess Mikhail

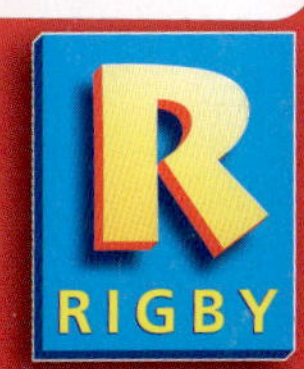

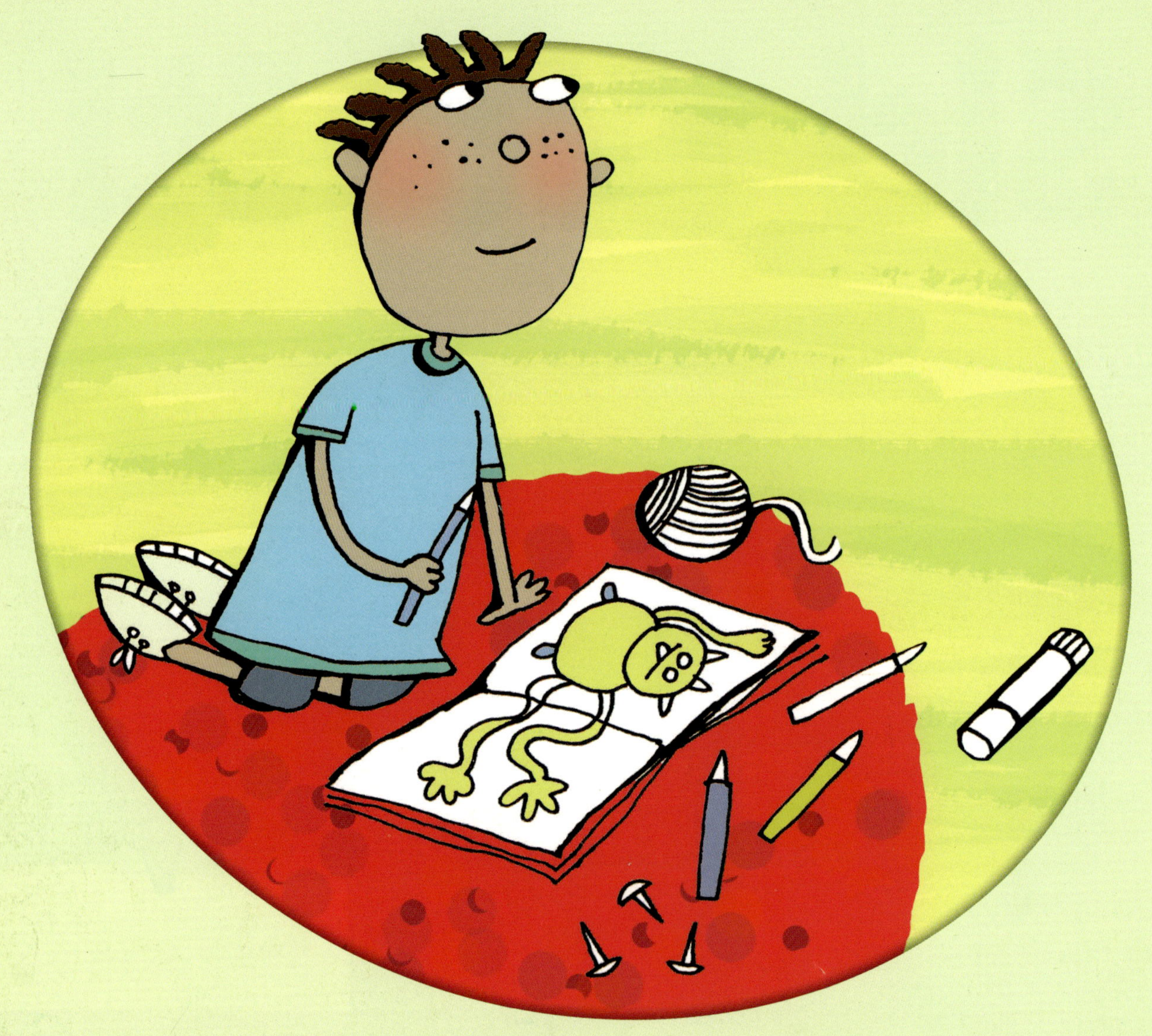

Sid

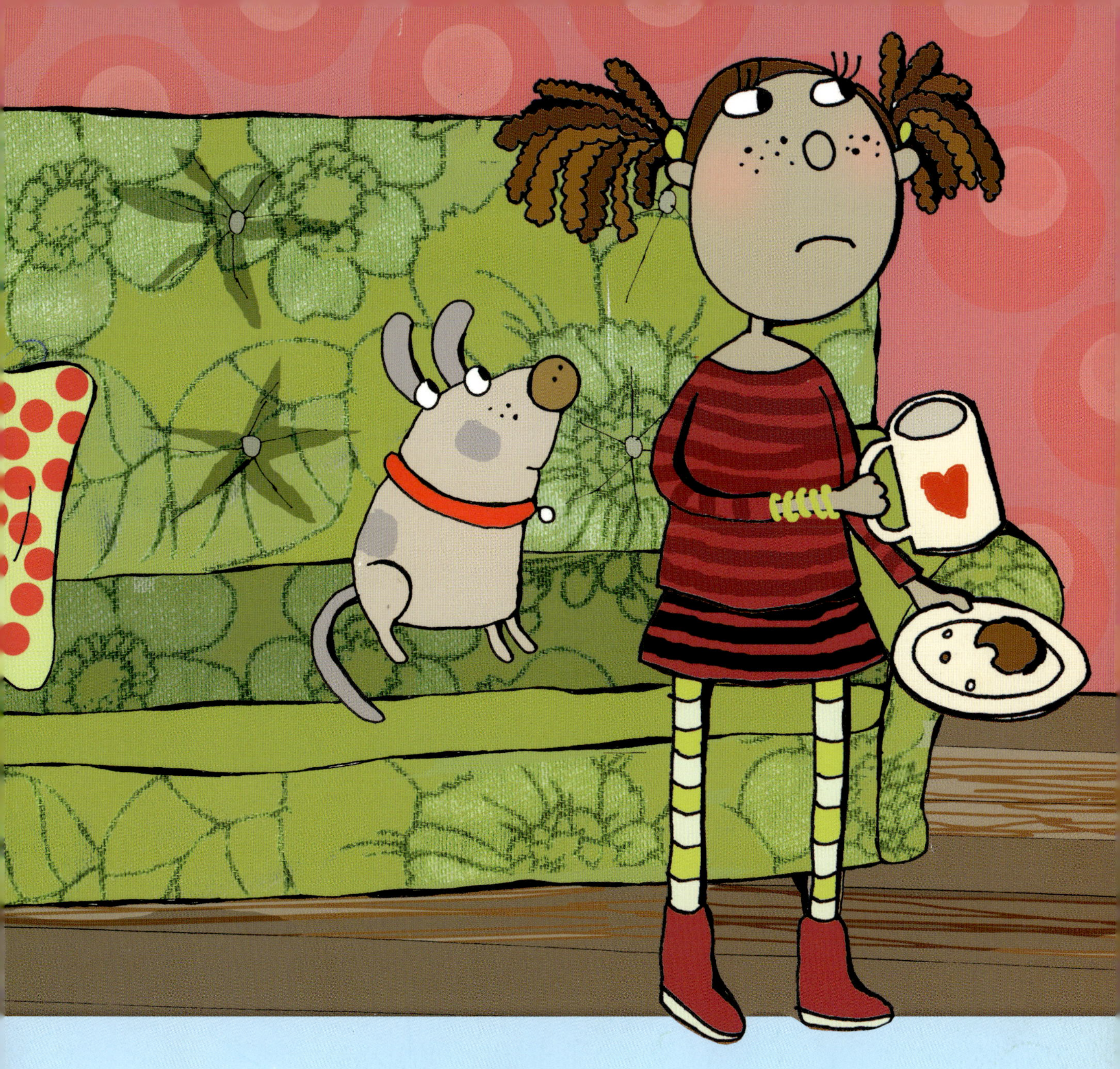

Sam

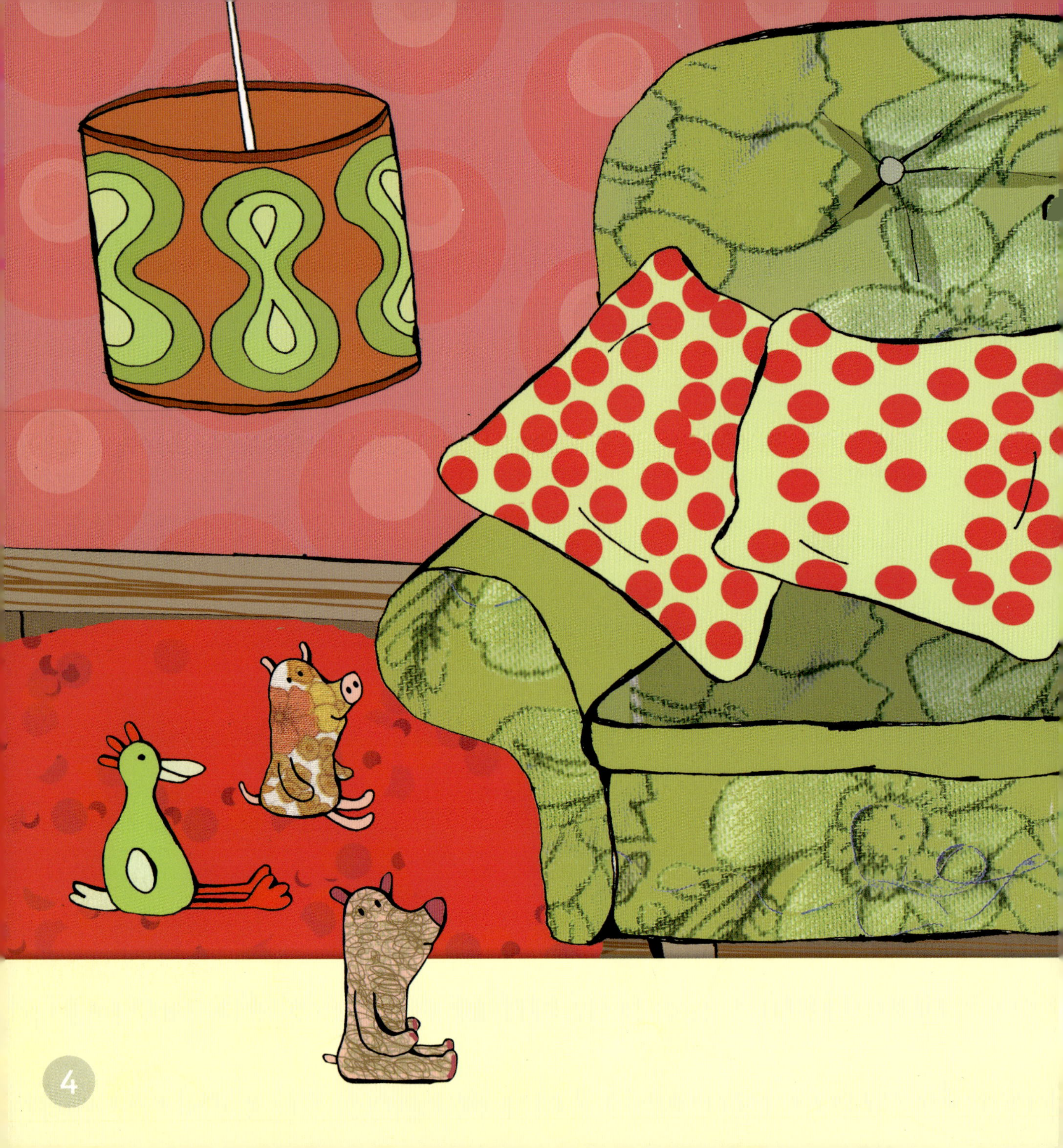

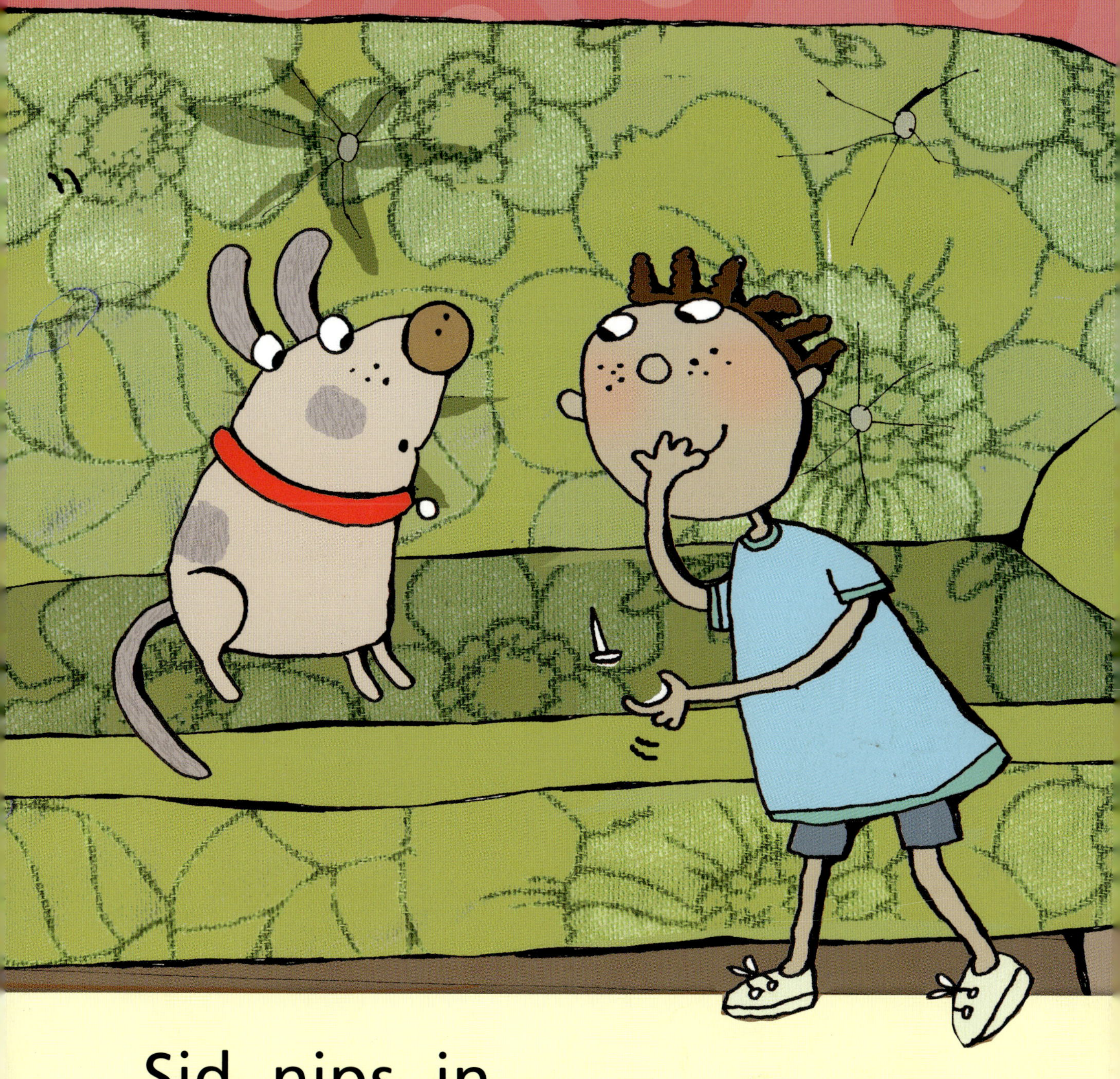

Sid nips in.

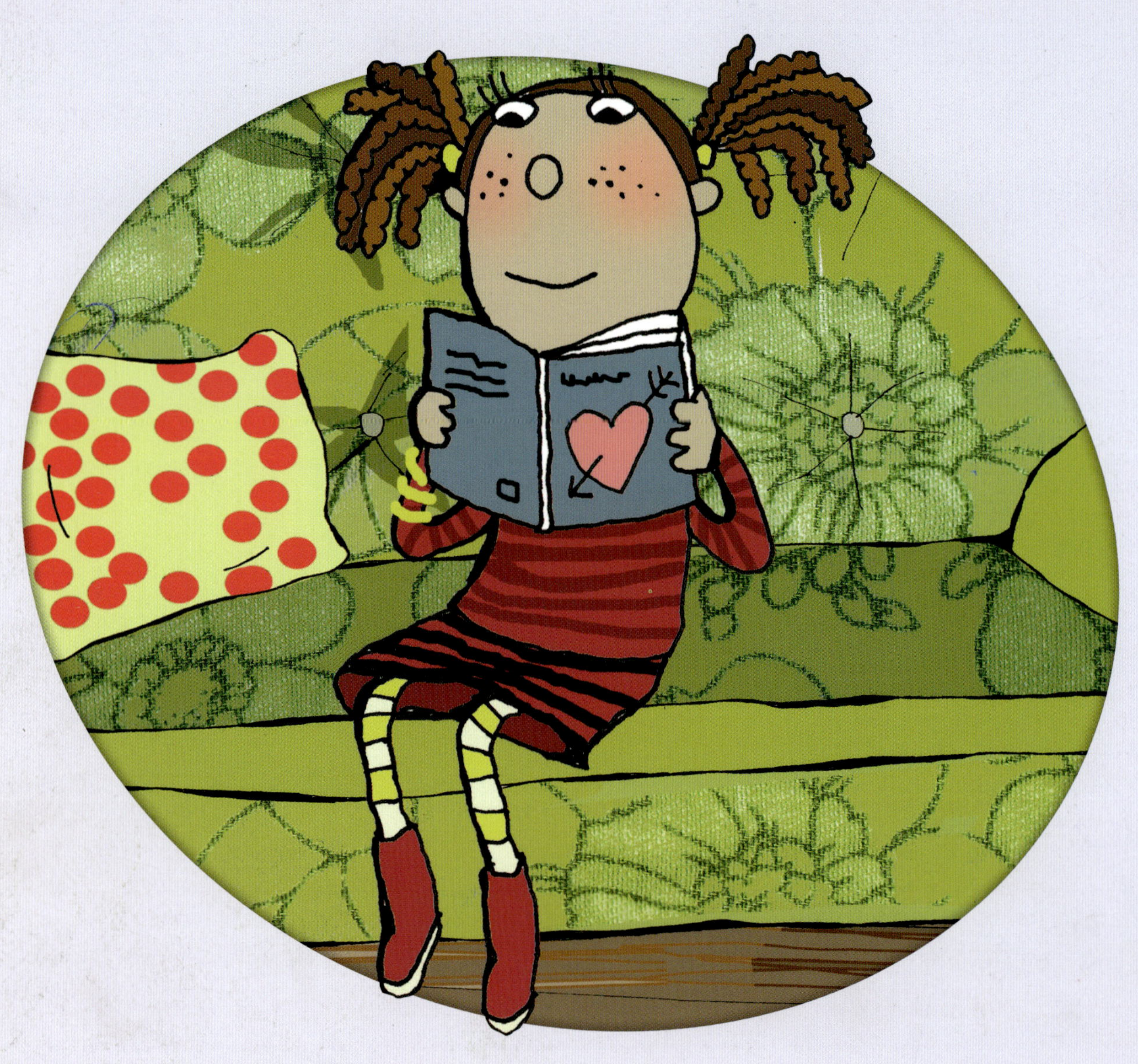

Sam sits.

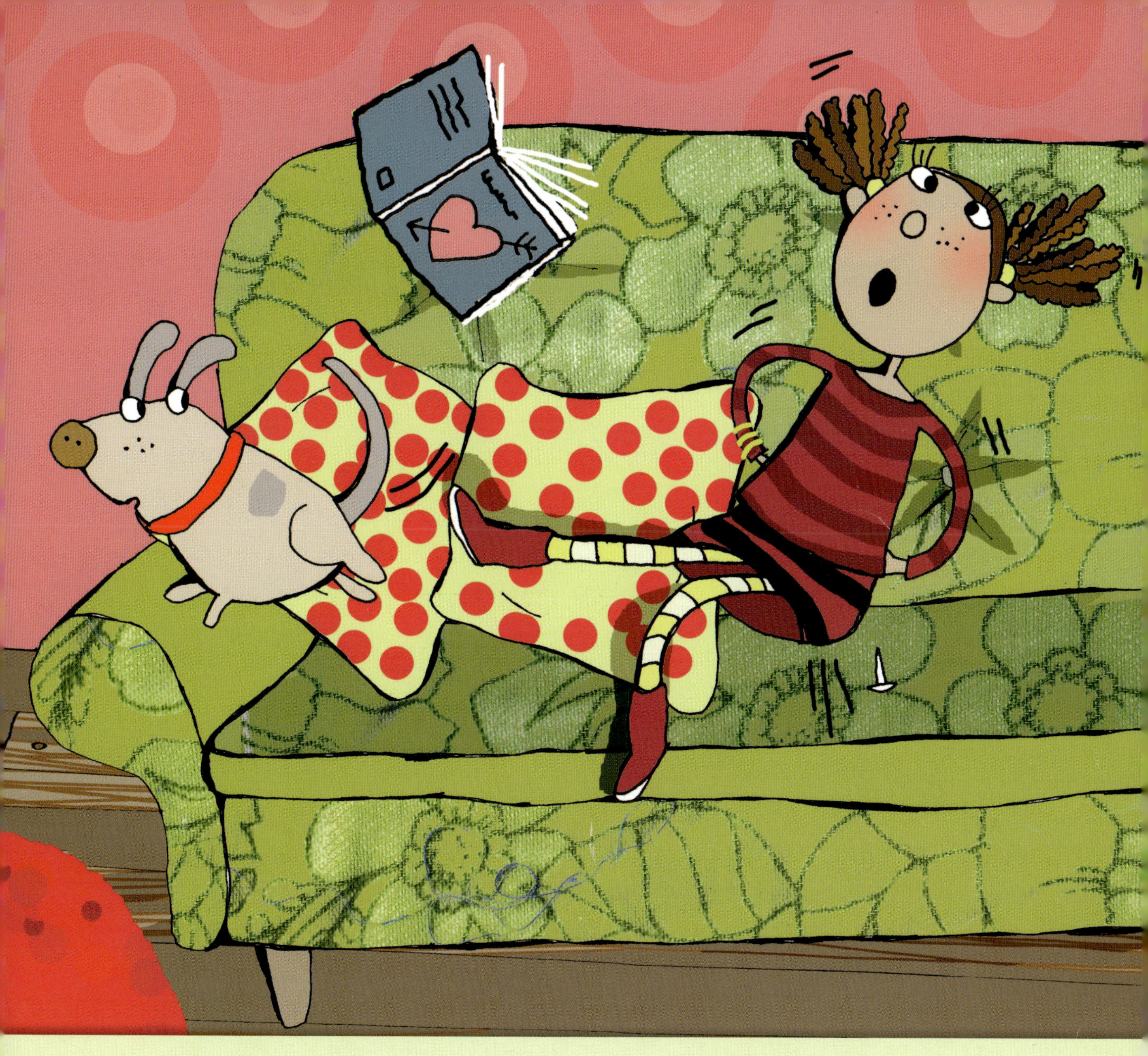

Sam is mad.

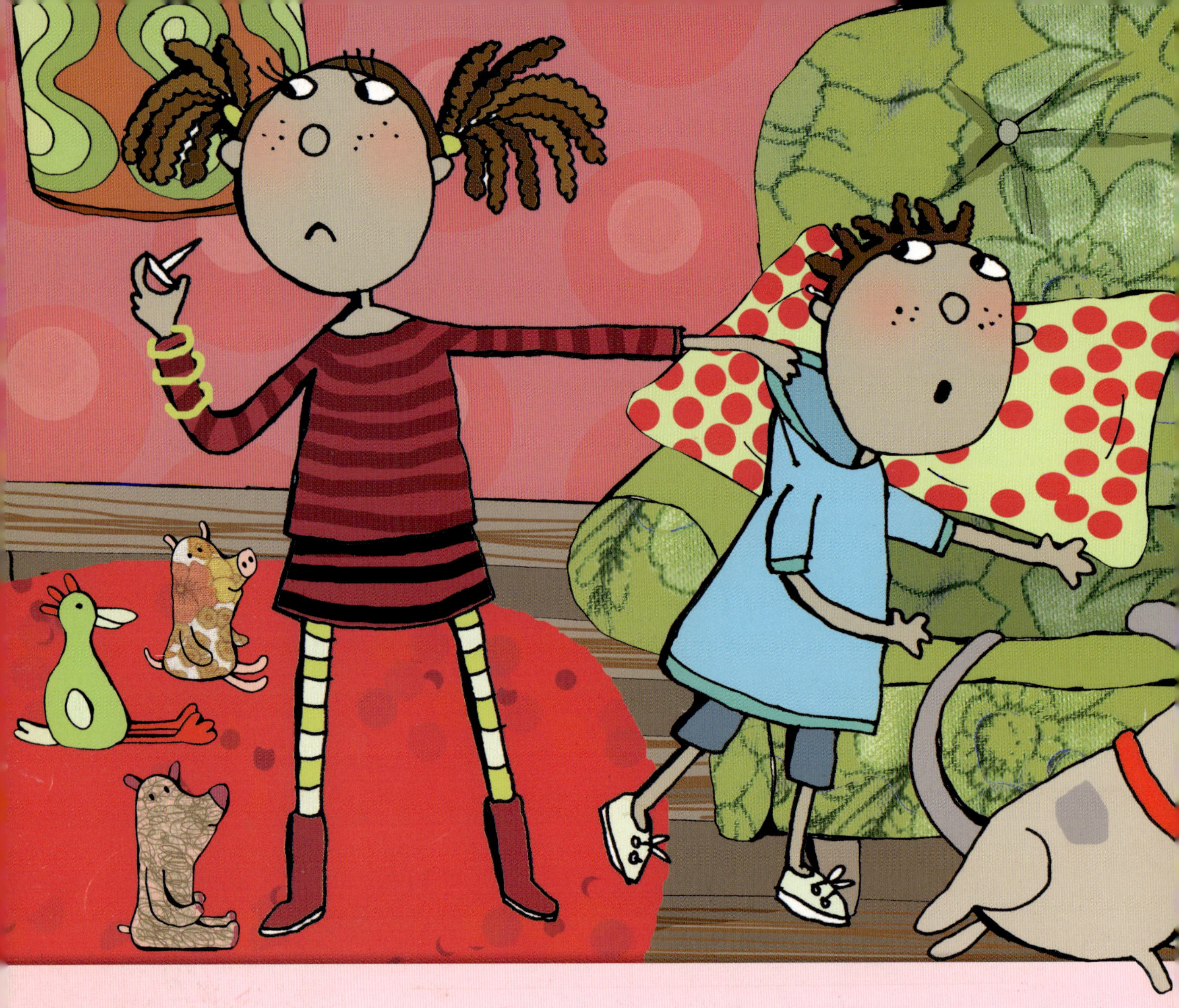

It is a pin!
Sid did it!